I Accept You As You Are!

by David Parker

Illustrated by Gioia Fiammenghi

SCHOLASTIC INC.

New York Toronto London Auckland Sydney
Mexico City New Delhi Hong Kong Buenos Aires

To my sister Yvonne — who treats everyone as family,
and to my "older sister" Carol — who shows everyone
they are important.
— D.P.

To Tristan and Milan
— G.F.C.

ISBN 0-439-62811-3

Text copyright © 2004 by David Parker
Illustrations copyright © 2004 by Gioia Fiammenghi
All rights reserved. Published by Scholastic Inc.
SCHOLASTIC, THE BEST ME I CAN BE™ Readers, and associated logos
are trademarks and/or registered trademarks of Scholastic Inc.

12 11 10 9 8 7 6   4 5 6 7 8 9/0

Printed in the U.S.A.
First printing, March 2004

There are so many children in my school who I see.
Sometimes I wish there was only me.

I want to be special, important—just me.
With so many others, how can that be?

Some children have different color skin.
Some are tall, and some are thin.

I may not know their names or their family,
but all the children who I see are important just like me.

Some wear colorful clothes from a far-off land.
Some speak in languages I don't understand.

Some act silly, and some act sad.
Some act grumpy, and some act glad.

I may not know their names or their family,
but all the children who I see are important just like me.

Some children read out loud, and some read quietly.
Some children play alone, and others play with me.

Some see with their fingers or talk with their hands.
Other children ride because they cannot stand.

I may not know their names or their family,
but all the children who I see are important just like me.

Some children like to dance, and some like to sing.
Some like to throw a ball. We all like different things.

All of us are different, and it makes me want to say,
"Each one of us is special, and I like it just that way."

There are so many children in my school who I see.
They all are so important—just like me!

Name some things that are different
and alike about you and your classmates.